Squirrel Says
Thank You

written by Dr. Mary Manz Simon
illustrated by Kathy Couri

© 2003 Mary Manz Simon. © 2003 Standard Publishing, Cincinnati, Ohio. A division of Standex International Corporation.
All rights reserved. Sprout logo is a trademark of Standard Publishing. First Virtues™ is a trademark of Standard Publishing.
Printed in Italy. Project editor: Jennifer Holder. Design: Robert Glover and Suzanne Jacobson. Scripture quoted from the *HOLY
BIBLE, Contemporary English Version.* Copyright © 1995 by the American Bible Society. Used by permission. ISBN 0-7847-1415-0

09 08 07 06 05 04 03   9 8 7 6 5 4 3 2 1

**Standard
Publishing**

cincinnati, ohio

www.standardpub.com

Squirrel, Squirrel,
share today,
what the Bible
has to say…

I say "Thank you"
every day
for the good
that comes my way.

I count blessings:
one, two, three.
God gives such
great things to me.

Ice cream tastes
so nice and sweet.
I thank God
for this cold treat.

I thank God
for big, tall trees,
and the cooling
autumn breeze.

And when snowflakes
flutter by,
I thank God
I'm warm and dry.

I am glad for family, too—people who say "I love you."

These are blessings
big and small.
Thank you, God,
for giving all.

God shares
each of these with me.
I say "Thank you"
gratefully.

"We thank you, our God,
and praise you."
1 Chronicles 29:13

Thankfulness Thankfulness Thankfulness

Thankfulness Thankfulness Thankfulness

Thankfulness Thankfulness Thankfulness

Thankfulness Thankfulness Thankfulness

Thankfulness Thankfulness Thankfulness

Thankfulness Thankfulness Thankfulness

Thankfulness Thankfulness Thankfulness